Published by Brown Watson (Leicester) Ltd.

© 1986 Rand McNally & Company
Printed and bound in the German Democratic Republic

# NONI the Christmas Reindeer

By Daphne Doward Hogstrom
Illustrated by June Goldsborough

**Brown Watson**

ENGLAND

Noni could fly faster and farther
than any other reindeer at the North
Pole, but she was never allowed to
pull Santa's sleigh.

"You are too small," Santa told her. "I need big, strong deer to haul my heavy load. You stay at home and guard the stable, day by day."

But it was lonely guarding the reindeer stable every day. Most of the time, Dasher, Dancer, Prancer, Vixen, Comet, Cupid, Dunder and

Blitzen were off in the fields and
forests, running and jumping and
getting ready for their Christmas
Eve ride.

And, of course, on Christmas Eve
itself, they flew through the sky
with Santa's sack.

"Surely I can help Santa, too,"

thought Noni, one especially lonely
Christmas when even her friends,
the stable mice, had left her to sleep
together in the warm soft straw.

"If I cannot help *pull* Santa's
sleigh, then perhaps I can help
*fill* it !" she thought. "I will fly to
the farthest corners of the world

and find new and wonderful toys
for the girls and boys."

And, on the very first day after
Christmas, truc to her word, off she
went to the four wide ends of the
earth!

"Good!" said Santa, when Noni found a little wooden clown that turned and tumbled, and stood upon his head in a hoop.

"Great!" said Santa, when she found a tiny china chicken that squawled and squawked and laid a china egg.

"Grand!" said Santa, when she discovered a big silver robot—who walked and talked and stared with fiery eyes!

In the farthest nooks and crannies

Tremendous!" said Santa, when a
...e in a far-distant kingdom gave
...co cat that swung upon a swing.

of the world, Noni fou
more wonderful toys

"Marvellous!" said
queen in a faraway c
teddy bear that bala

"T
princ
a cal

"Terrific!" cried Santa, when a king in a palace on a pinnacle gave a painted horse that pranced around a ring.

All year long, Noni found more and more toys for Santa's sack.

She found little tin trains that
puffed and whistled.

She found little tin planes that
flit and flew.

She found a fire truck with ever-

ready water, and a toy box with
ninety-five toys.

She found paints made with colours
from the rainbow, and a book brushed
with stardust and dew.

She found a flute that played tunes forever, and a crystal ball that showed the sun and moon.

Finally, on a faraway mountain in a meadow—she found a magician making dolls that danced and sang!

"Perfect!" cried Santa at last, on Christmas Eve. "But my sack is filled to overflowing, so I'll need your help to guard my heavy load."

And, almost faster than Noni could
fly—he hitched her up *behind* his
waiting sleigh!

"Please watch out and warn for
falling toys," he called, as he
climbed to his seat beside the sack.
Dasher, Dancer, Prancer, Vixen,

Comet, Cupid, Dunder and Blitzen
flew happily at the front of Santa's
sleigh, steering their way through
the stars.

But Noni flew happily at the *back* of Santa's sleigh, watching for dolls that might tumble through the darkness, or for clowns that might topple through the clouds.

"I'll never be lonely again," she said—thinking of all the toys she would find for next Christmas, too!